Mr Gumpy's Outing

John Burningham

PUFFIN BOOKS

Other Puffin picture books by John Burningham

MR GUMPY'S MOTOR CAR
GRANPA

PUFFIN BOOKS

Published by the Penguin Group
Penguin Books Ltd, 27 Wrights Lane, London W8 5TZ, England
Penguin Putnam Inc., 345 Hudson Street, New York, New York 10014, USA
Penguin Books Australia Ltd, Ringwood, Victoria, Australia
Penguin Books Canada Ltd, 10 Alcorn Avenue, Toronto, Ontario, Canada M4V 3B2
Penguin Books (NZ) Ltd, Private Bag 102902, Auckland, New Zealand

Penguin Books Ltd, Registered Offices: Harmondsworth, Middlesex, England

First published in Great Britain by Jonathan Cape 1973
First published in the USA by Thomas Y. Crowell Company 1976
Published in Picture Puffins 1979
29 30 28

Printed in Italy by Printer Trento srl

This is Mr Gumpy.

Mr Gumpy owned a boat and his house
was by a river.

One day Mr Gumpy went out in his boat.

"May we come with you?" said the children.

"Yes," said Mr Gumpy,
"if you don't squabble."

"Can I come along, Mr Gumpy?"
said the rabbit.

"Yes, but don't hop about."

"I'd like a ride," said the cat.

"Very well," said Mr Gumpy.
"But you're not to chase the rabbit."

"Will you take me with you?" said the dog.

"Yes," said Mr Gumpy.
"But don't tease the cat."

"May I come, please, Mr Gumpy?"
said the pig.

"Very well, but don't muck about."

"Have you a place for me?" said the sheep.

"Yes, but don't keep bleating."

"Can we come too?" said the chickens.

"Yes, but don't flap," said Mr Gumpy.

"Can you make room for me?" said the calf.

"Yes, if you don't trample about."

"May I join you, Mr Gumpy?" said the goat.

"Very well, but don't kick."

For a little while they all went along happily but then...

The goat kicked

The calf trampled

The chickens flapped

The sheep bleated

The pig mucked about

The dog teased the cat

The cat chased the rabbit

The rabbit hopped

The children squabbled

The boat tipped ...

and into the water they fell.

Then Mr Gumpy and the goat and the calf and the chickens and the sheep and the pig and the dog and the cat and the rabbit and the children all swam to the bank and climbed out to dry in the hot sun.

"We'll walk home across the fields," said Mr Gumpy. "It's time for tea."

"Goodbye," said Mr Gumpy.
"Come for a ride another day."